Lisa Horstman

Squawking Matilda

Marshall Cavendish Children

Marshall Cavendish Corporation
99 White Plains Road
Tarrytown, NY 10591
www.marshallcavendish.us/kids

This book is a work of fiction. Names, characters, places, and incidents are products of the author's imagination and are used fictitiously. Any resemblance to actual events or locales or persons, living or dead, is entirely coincidental.

Library of Congress Cataloging-in-Publication Data

Horstman, Lisa.
Squawking Matilda / by Lisa Horstman.
p. cm.
Summary: Mae likes starting projects but never seems to finish them, and so when Aunt Susan asks her to take care of a feisty chicken Mae is soon distracted, then must find a way to make up for her neglect before Aunt Susan's visit.
ISBN 978-0-7614-5463-2
[1. Chickens—Fiction. 2. Responsibility—Fiction. 3. Aunts—Fiction. 4. Farm life—Fiction.] I. Title.
PZ7.H7914Squ 2008
[E]—dc22
2008003657

Editor: Robin Benjamin
Printed in China
First edition
10 9 8 7 6 5 4 3 2 1

This book is for The Three Glones, who always cleaned up my project messes, and for Dave. It is also for Andrea, with thanks.

AUTHOR NOTE: Each puppet illustration in this book began as a stainless steel inner scaffolding, or armature. A flexible body was created around it with wool felting, and hands and heads were sculpted and baked with polymer clay. The finished posable puppet was dressed in clothing either knit or sewn by hand and then photographed against a neutral background. Color was added digitally to the image of the puppet and superimposed against a backdrop that was painted earlier and scanned separately. Then the artist took a nap.

Dear Mae,
How is my favorite

One day Mae received a note from Aunt Susan:

Dear Mae,

How is my favorite niece?

(Mae giggled at the joke: she was Aunt Susan's *only* niece.)

I have a special job for you. I know how you love projects. One of my new chickens doesn't like it on my farm. Maybe she would like it better on yours. Would you look after her? She might even lay some eggs for you. Wouldn't that be fun?

Love,

Aunt Susan

"A new project!" Mae squealed to her cat (whose name was Cat).

Mae was always looking for a new project. Last month she decided to make a special litter-box cover for Cat. Then Cat could have privacy. And space. And a place to read. (If only cats *could* read.)

But before Mae finished the litter box, something else caught her attention.

In the dark of night, everyone in the family was constantly tripping over the dog (whose name was Dog). "Aha!" thought Mae. "A little glow-in-the-dark paint on his sweater will do the trick." But then Dog couldn't sleep. . . .

Before Mae could figure out a better solution, a new project came up. The cows needed her help. Their poor udders looked so cold when it was chilly outside. Mae to the rescue!

moooooooooooooo!

Mae learned that cows do not like to have their udders covered up. The cows refused to move.

But now . . . taking care of an unhappy chicken? This seemed like a *really* special and important project. Mae had to do a bit of fast talking to convince her parents that this was a project she could handle.

"Mom and Dad, I can do this I know I can please say yes I'll take good care of her I'll check on her every day I won't let Aunt Susan down please please oh please let me take care of this CHICKEN!" blurted Mae.

And what do you know, Mae's parents said, "Okay."

On a bright, clear day, Aunt Susan's package arrived!

Mae opened the package and out popped the sassiest, smartest, most beee-yoo-tiful chicken she had ever seen.

"Now that's a chicken with attitude!" said Mae's dad. "Are you sure you can handle her?"

Mae was eager to try.

"Yes!" she declared.

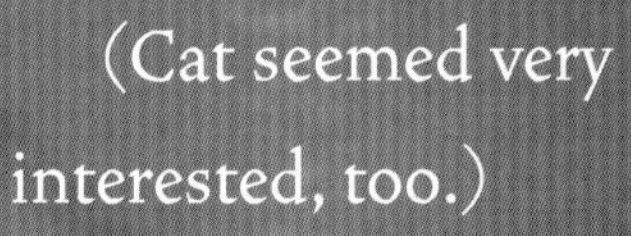

(Cat seemed very interested, too.)

"I'll call her Matilda," said Mae. It was a dignified, proud name for such a proud, dignified chicken (not to mention, scrappy).

But how *do* you handle a chicken? Mae had always been too busy with her projects to help out in the henhouse. She had to learn how to feed Matilda, make sure she had fresh water to drink . . . and clean her coop.

"Whoo-*eee*!" said Mae each time she cleaned it. It was stinky—*really* stinky.

Work, work, work! It was almost too much for Mae. There were times when Matilda was *too* scrappy,

when she refused to eat, when her pen was stinkier than stinky—

those were the moments when Mae almost gave up.

In a way, Mae *did* give up. There was always something else that needed her attention. . . .

Like building a clubhouse
for the sheep . . .

or giving Cat a
new hairdo . . .

or making a fabulous
new hat for Dog. . . .

And then nobody took special care of Matilda. None of the other chickens liked having a new chicken around—especially one as proud (and scrappy) as she was.

Matilda felt forgotten.

One day some of her feathers fell out,

then a few more,

and a few more until . . .

Matilda had almost no feathers at all.

That got Mae's attention, all right. "Poor Matilda!" thought Mae. "She looks embarrassed. And cold."

Mae fussed and fretted, thought and thought. "Well, to start, I have to make sure she is warm," Mae decided.

Mae collected feathers from the henhouse. She took her glue bottle and, one by one, glued the feathers back on Matilda.

Matilda did NOT like the glue. She squawked and tried to rub it off.

But Mae had already moved on to another project. Her pet mouse needed new shoes. . . .

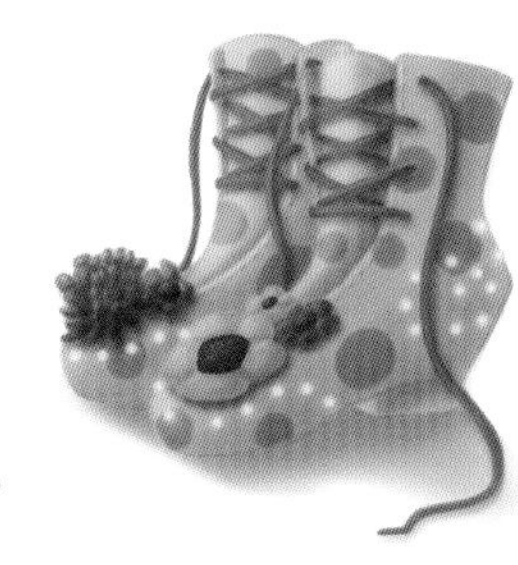

The next morning Mae went to feed Matilda, but Matilda was gone.

Mae looked all over the henhouse,

and in the barn,

and under the porch.

Matilda was nowhere to be found.

To make matters worse, a note from Aunt Susan arrived:

Dear Mae,

I will be coming for a visit at the end of the month. How is Matilda? I'm sure you are taking good care of her. I can't wait to see what a great job you've done! See you soon.

Love,

Aunt Susan

Mae had three weeks to make everything better. She didn't want to let Aunt Susan down, and she really did want Matilda to be a happy chicken.

And so, first thing first, Mae needed to find Matilda. After a long search, Mae went back to the henhouse. *Aha!* Finally, there was Matilda. “Where have you been?” asked Mae. But, of course, Matilda didn’t answer.

Matilda had shaken off most of the feathers. “I need to find a better way to keep you warm,” said Mae.

She scooped up Matilda and carried her to the house. Matilda pecked at her hands the entire way. *Nothing* was ever easy with Matilda.

How would she keep Matilda warm? Mae fussed and fretted some more until . . . *"Aha!"* yelled Mae. Using leftover scraps from other projects, she made something very special for Matilda—a chicken jacket! She even made her a chicken hat.

Matilda did NOT like the hat.

Pu-KAAAAWK!

squawked Matilda.

Clink! Clink! Clink! There were so many shells and coins and charms sewn and pasted onto the jacket that Matilda *clinked* each time she moved, and if she didn't *clink*, she *clanked*.

But Matilda liked the warm, noisy jacket. She proudly *clinked* and *clanked* all around the henhouse, showing off to the other chickens. (They were not very impressed.)

"That's a jacket with attitude," thought Mae.

Over the next few weeks, Mae worked very hard to take care of Matilda—she even cleaned the smelly coop every day. She had never worked this hard on one project before.

And Matilda seemed happier. She didn't squawk so much, and she wasn't so feisty.

Mae could see tiny new feathers poking through Matilda's jacket. Some of the coins and charms had started to fall off. Mae realized that soon Matilda wouldn't need the jacket anymore.

At last the big day arrived. Aunt Susan was here! "I'm sorry, Aunt Susan, I didn't take good care of Matilda at first and she was sad and her feathers fell out but I made her a warm noisy jacket and even a hat but she didn't like the hat and I took better care of her and now she's happy!" blurted Mae.

Aunt Susan said, "That's great, Mae! I'd love to see her."

But Matilda was nowhere to be found. Again!

They looked everywhere. They even checked the henhouse twice. No Matilda.

"Hmm," said Aunt Susan. No one said anything for a minute. Then Mae spied a piece of the chicken jacket on the ground. There were more pieces leading into the woods. Mae stared at Cat—but Cat looked innocent.

They followed the trail . . .

and followed it . . .

and followed it . . .

. . . to the end. And there, inside a hollow tree, was Matilda—safe and snug in a nest made from her jacket.

She was sitting on one perfect egg.

"Aha!" said Mae. "So that's what you've been up to. I've never seen a chicken lay an egg in a tree before."

Mrrrow! said Cat. (Neither had he.)

Aunt Susan said, "Well done, Mae! Do you know what I think? It wasn't the jacket that did the trick. It was all that love and care you gave Matilda. That was all she needed to be happy. And that's what she needed to lay an egg."

Mae thought about this. "I think maybe you're right. It was a lot of work, but this was my best project yet!" Then she thought about it some more. . . .

“But I’ll make her a new jacket, anyway,” added Mae. “Just in case.”

Squawk! said Matilda.